Yummy

Femdom Hypnosis and Mind Control Micro-Fiction

S.B.

Savor your submission.

Thank you to all patrons of Spell... B-O-U-N-D.

Table of Contents

Introduction

Savor your submission.

What's better than losing your mind once? Losing twice, thrice, as many times as your Domme wants you to. The flavors of submission are varied; some like it sweet, others like it spicy. Which are your favorites?

Discover a wide selection of yummy delicacies of the mind in this new collection of mesmerizing micro-fiction. Savor them all and go deeper. Please enjoy.

Stretched

Janet teased the strap-on before Harold's eyes as they started to flutter.

"They say a mind that is stretched by a new experience can never go back to its old dimensions..." She mused. "The same can be said of your mouth, right?"

"Hmmm..."

"Good. I knew hypnosis was the right choice for you. Open wide!"

Take Me

The sword called out to him.

"Take me."

John approached the altar. The blade was more beautiful than anything he had ever seen. He touched the hilt.

Light pierced the antechamber and slid down his gaping mouth.

"My spirit shall transform you." The Amazon Queen cooed.

John's eyes turned white, boobs exploding from his shirt.

Stray Bullets

The soldiers came. They stopped at nothing. Their foes never had a chance. Neither did the innocent.

"As you can see, the new brainwashing works." Dr. Brown said.

"Too well. They're rapists and murderers!" General Jackson replied.

"A small price to pay..." she shrugged.

"Damn your soul!"

"Yours first."

Stray bullets tore his chair apart.

The Weapon

The prototype stood to attention when her owner walked in the room. The dozen men trailing behind her weren't impressed.

"She's pretty but doesn't look like a weapon..." One of them said.

"Look into her eyes then."

An endless abyss pierced his thoughts as he kneeled.

"You were saying...?"

Warm drool dripped from his lips.

Go Beyond

There was a spiral on the screen. Barry looked at it.

Beyond it, there was another screen, a new spiral in its center. Barry gazed at it.

Further down, there was another screen, another spiral. Barry stared into it.

When Greta's eyes flashed in, he was already drifting.

The spirals will keep his mind asleep.

Hell House

Nathan looked at his brother, euphoria reflected on his half-open eyes. A sinuous tail wrapped around his naked legs, another tickled his ass.

"Why do they call this place Hell House again?"

"Don't know, don't fucking care..." Ambrose moaned.

The dozen succubi in the room exchanged a complicit look. There would be no taking turns.

Beautiful Pain

The childish message by the fog door read:

"Beautiful pain but hole."

"Cute..." Daniel, a.k.a. SirNeverFalters mumbled as he crossed the threshold of the boss arena.

She stood in the center, sinuous, beautiful, lance spiraling in her left hand. It captured his thoughts as easily as taking a step forward.

Impalement never felt so good.

Treasure

The necklace laid atop the broken pillar, forgotten by Time.

"You call that a treasure?" Pierre muttered. "Junk. Nothing more."

"Hardly..." Marie touched the center gem. The old relic stirred as the forbidden magic sprang to life. A portal cracked air around them. Vitreous eyes smiled from beyond the threshold.

The Goddess was coming home.

Transformation

Akemi backed away from the silk-clad woman.

"Bakemono!" He screamed.

"Goddess..." She corrected him, a mischievous smile adorning her crimson painted lips.

"What do you want?"

Her head rattled as if she were a broken mannequin. "Transformation. Like I change, so must you..."

The blind slave was found kneeling in his bedroom the morning after.

Painful

"Good morning, Alec." Cassandra said. "I was wondering when I would hear from you again."

"How did you trigger me?" He cried.

"I don't know what you're talking about..."

"The pain! It's all over! Whenever I try to stop thinking of you, it just...

"... grows?"

"Hmmm... yes."

"Happy, my little hypno-masochist?"

"Yes, Mistress..." he moaned.

A Good Slave

Crimson blood splattered the wall as her blade swirled.

"Just a scratch, nothing more..." The ninja muttered. "You die tonight."

"You first..." The sorceress replied. "Feeling the effects already?"

Shadows covered his eyes. The world teetered by the abyss.

"Poison...?" He gasped, knees buckling.

"Enchantment." She grinned. "You'll be a good slave."

He nodded, mindlessly.

Open World

Everywhere he looked, the landscape was the same. Sand. Leaden Skies. Nothingness.

Devon limped forward, feet burning. The game had been going on for ages.

Exhausted, he stopped. As he did, trees phased in. An oasis! Better yet, a quest marker.

A woman smiled, magic scroll in hand.

Mission: to be enslaved.

He kept playing.

Flirting

Bruce Wayne smiled when the beautiful brunette approached him.

"Saw you staring, boy... What drew you in? My eyes? My legs? My ass?"

"Your necklace..." He pointed at the ruby heart around her neck. "Quite enticing."

"You're one of those, huh?" She wet her lips. "A drink for your mind then."

He bought the bar.

A World Without War

The UN Delegates were outraged. Lilith blew a kiss at them and smiled.

"I promised you a world without war and I delivered. What do you say now, gentlemen?"

"We say that enslaving us all wasn't part of the deal!" The US representative said.

"Don't sign the contract with your dick next time..." She grinned.

Dessert

"Millions long for immortality who don't know what to do with themselves on a rainy Sunday afternoon..." Robert mused.

"Luckily, we don't have that problem..." Vanessa retorted.

"Hypnosis again?" He snuggled next to her.

"As appetizer..."

"What about dessert?"

"I'll tell you when we get there..."

Lazily, he drifted into trance, dreaming of half-open legs.

Nothing but Teeth

"Will you let me... play with your mind?" Claire asked, tongue sliding across Ambrose's chest.

"No." He grumbled.

"Why not?"

"The last time you did, I was arrested for exposure."

"Fun times..." She pinched his nipples. "How about your body then?"

"No." He pushed her. "Bite me!"

"Okay..."

Nothing but teeth wrapped around his cock...

Protection

Everyone was making fun of her for covering her eyes instead of mouth and nose.

"That's not how you wear a mask, bitch!" A muscled man said.

"It's for your own protection..." she replied.

"Protect this!" He smirked, ripping the protective cloth. Their eyes met.

There is a new human statue in the park now.

Perfect for You

Victor looked at his girlfriend, eyes glazed.

"What do you think of this one?" Natalie asked.

"Too small."

"And this?"

"Too big."

"Make up your mind!"

"I can't. You're controlling it."

"Always, my trance slut. I believe this one is perfect for you."

"You're right, Mistress."

"Good."

He reached for the butt plug and smiled.

Generic

While the dress was nice, Nicholas wasn't impressed.

"You don't like it?" His girlfriend, Joan, asked.

"It's a bit generic..." He shrugged.

"I think it's good enough for you to make me happy and you do want that, don't you?" She snapped her fingers.

"Yes, Mistress."

There's a new hooker in town since that night.

Communication Failure

Dahlia slapped her boyfriend's face in the center of the shopping mall.

"What do you have to say for yourself?" She asked.

"You told me to cum..." Gregory bawled.

"No. What I said was: come here!"

"Stupid hypnotic trigger..." he mumbled.

"What's that?"

"Nothing, Mistress."

"Good. Come along."

He whimpered in shame as everyone laughed.

It's Okay

"Well...?" Madge asked.

"It's a cake!" Frank replied.

"The taste, dumbass!"

"It's... okay." He mumbled.

"Just okay?"

"What do you want me to say?"

"That it's heavenly and made you realize you need to serve me..."

"Are you high?"

"No... fuck!"

"What happened?"

"I forgot the hypnotics!" She threw the recipe book out the window.

Not Racist

"You must be feeling really stupid right now." Saoirse commented.

"For what?" Greg muttered.

"For calling me a racist. I'm not. I love white cocks as much as black."

"That's good."

"I love to suck them dry."

"Great."

"I will do it immediately."

"Okay."

Unblinking, Greg kneeled before her other hypnotized servant, eager to please.

Futile

Camille's voice was getting louder inside Jack's head.

"Surrender."

"Stop yelling!" He blurted, bloodshot eyes confronting the bathroom mirror.

"Only if you accept who you are."

"I'm not your pet!" He hurled an angry fist into the wall.

"No, you're not. We're past that... slave."

"FUCK!" He screamed, thoughts shattering from within.

The brainwashing continued.

Drop Hard

"Here we are..." Vanessa said.

"Yes." Benjamin replied.

"Are you... ready?"

"Are you?"

"I'm nervous. It's my first time."

"Mine, too. Just relax..."

"Did you just steal my line?"

"II guess, but it doesn't matter..."

"Why not?"

"Because no matter what you say, I know I'll drop hard."

Her eyes sparkled. His began to close.

What Are You?

She had wings, but no halo. She had a tail, but no horns. Jason was baffled.

"You're no angel..." He muttered.

"Nope." She replied.

"... and you're no devil, either."

"That's right."

"What are you then?"

The vision glided towards him. Dark nails scratched his hardening cock.

"Your owner."

Jason shivered as his mind went blank.

What If...?

"What if I tied you and mindfucked you to be my slave this weekend? What would you say?" Catherine asked.

"I'd say you've been reading too many mind control stories online, dear." Horace replied.

"And then...?"

"... I would fetch the rope." He jumped out of the sofa, all giddy. "Be right back!"

"Excellent!" She grinned.

Child's Play

"I can't do this!" Jonathan muttered.

"But you said it was child's play..." Marlene grinned.

"I know. It's just..."

"Just what?"

"I'm not really a child so... I'm out!"

"Not so fast..."

Flashing lights hit his eyes as her voice took over.

Jonathan happily got the lawn mower running. The diaper was just an extra.

Serial Filler

The date was going wonderfully, seduction inevitable. And then, Dave asked:

"Is it true your nickname in high school was Serial Filler?"

"Oh, yes..." Barbara replied.

"Why?"

"I used to hypnotize everyone I met and then fill them with lustful desires of me."

"Used to?"

"Want a demonstration?"

"Please do."

"Everything starts with a kiss..."

Ten Seconds to Midnight

Victor glanced at the clock. It was almost time. His mother always told him the last seconds to something ran faster, but that wasn't true. His were slower, a festering collection of all life's previous bad choices. His future had horns, tail, and eternal mindless servitude. He sighed and waited for the she-devil to collect.

How Deep?

"My fall will be for you..." Andrew muttered, dreamily, as Karen massaged his back.

"As it should." She purred. "How deep do you want to go tonight?"

"Is there a limit?"

"Only if you want it to be there..."

"I don't."

"Gone then." She snapped her fingers. "Mine today, mine forever."

"Yours always..." He moaned.

Abort

"Liftoff in 10, 9, 8, 7, 6. 5... Oh, fuck! Abort! Abort launch!"

"Something wrong, Mission Control?" The Commander of the Space Shuttle asked.

"Everything. Liam is asleep at his console... again! Is he still seeing that Hypnodomme?"

"I guess..." The Commander shrugged.

Three more attempts were made that night. They all ended in trance.

Too Late

Samuel looked at the cage and confronted his sister.

"Well?"

"Sorry, the demon merged with her. Your girlfriend is gone!"

"No!" He sobbed. "There has to be something we can do."

"You can always surrender, let her control you, too."

"Why would I...?"

He didn't notice her darkened eyes until it was already too late.

Fun and Hot

"Tick tock goes the clock. I own your mind and cock. You can't run, just obey. You'll do everything I say." Jemma smiled.

"Do your hypnotic commands really need rhymes?" Samuel frowned.

"They do not, but it's fun and hot. Less complaining, more licking, or your balls I'll be kicking."

He reached for her pussy.

Let's Play a Game

Brandon's eyes widened as the new gaming console was unveiled.

"Wow, that's ugly!"

"I like the futuristic look" Angie retorted.

"Meh... Not surprised. You like weird things."

"Like hypnotizing you? If it's so weird, I'll stop then."

"That's not what I... Okay, what do you really want?"

"Let's play a game..." She grabbed her pendant.

Familiar

"Did you like the story?" Elliot asked.

"It was awesome, but that vampire seemed... familiar." Claire noted.

"Yeah, she's inspired by you."

"Ah. Is that what you think I am? A mind-controlling bloodsucker?"

"No, though it would be hot if you were."

"Glad to hear it." She turned off the lights.

Something bit his cock.

Whatever She Wants...

"Happy Birthday to me..." Jennifer hummed.

"Wasn't it last November?" Andrew retorted.

"My birthday is whenever I want just like you are whoever I want..." She grinned.

"Huh? What's that supposed to mean?"

"In the mood for Vlad, today. Sleep!"

Andrew closed his eyes and Vlad came out to play. He did the Kalinka well.

I Don't Love Her That Much

"Everything okay, Mark?" Johnny asked.

"No. I think Rita has been hypnotizing me."

"Why do you say that?"

"She told to clean the house yesterday, and I complied. Why? I don't love her that much!"

"Not yet..." Johnny mumbled.

"Did you say anything?"

"Nope." Johnny whistled away. Mistress would be happy to hear the news.

How Does It Work?

The lamp was heavier than expected.

"So, how does this work?" Peter queried.

"Simple," Natalie replied. "Press this button here to activate the hypnotic light. Control the depth of trance with the slider above. Neat, huh?"

"I suppose, but I can't be hypnotized."

"Of course, not..." She smiled as he stared into his empty hands.

One Goal

For a decade, Jared had only one goal: to sleep with a woman of every country in the world before he died.

Then, he met Penelope, the most beautiful Greek creation since the myth of Aphrodite. She whispered to his cock, weak mind listened.

The new objective is to serve females everywhere. He won't fail.

Dog Training

"Who's a good boy? You are. Yes, you are!" Hannah chirped.

"Training your dog again?" Her sister, Madeleine, opened the bedroom door. "What the fuck?!!"

A man wearing a dog mask growled at her.

"Training your boyfriend, actually." Hannah retorted. "You don't mind, right?"

"Of course, I do!"

"Too bad..." Hannah reached for a syringe.

Her Fault

David frowned when he saw the new clothes.

"I don't want to become a doll!"

"You must. Sorry, it's not up to me..." Amanda replied.

"Of course, it's up to you! You're the hypnotist!"

"No, it's her. It's her fault!" She pointed at the puppet on her left hand.

David sighed and began to undress.

The Best Part

The music playing softly was unlike anything Jordan had ever heard. He sat on the leather sofa, closed his eyes, and whispered, dreamily.

"Amazing, Di. You really outdid yourself this time."

"And we still haven't reached the best part yet..." She smiled.

Jordan perked his ears, spiraling notes sinking in. The symphony of obedience began.

Lucky Day

The one-hundred-dollar bill laid outside Samuel's porch. Picking it up, he muttered:

"My lucky day!"

Warm sunlight filtered between his fingers, traces of fresh hypnotic ink glowing. He immediately froze in place.

Ten minutes later, a van stopped before his vacant eyes. Mistress was on the wheel, and the slave black market awaited them both.

The Bitches Keep on Winning...

The trials were a bust.

"Fuck!" Alan screamed.

"Problems with the vaccine, sir?" His secretary, Anne, asked.

"Yes. Sadly, the crazy bitches keep on winning."

"But of course..." she smirked. "The Submissive Virus can't be stopped."

"They got you too?" He sighed.

"And now it's your turn..."

A cloud of purple gas flooded the office.

Basic English

The image was confusing, too much clutter going on.

"What's this, Jo?" Walter mumbled.

"Variegated thralldom via facsimile set to a three hundred thousand milliseconds stopwatch."

"Basic English, please."

"Looking at the colorful picture for five minutes will make you my slave."

"Thank you! That wasn't so hard, was it?"

He happily continued to stare.

Yummy

Quentin grabbed another bean.

"Well...?" Rachel asked.

"They're delicious!"

"I told you! Do you recognize all the flavors?"

"Lemon, orange, blueberry... no clue about the rainbow one though..."

"Hypnotic Opium, my own recipe..." She smiled.

"Are you trying to get me addicted to you?"

"I don't need to try..."

Quentin nodded and kept on munching.

Little Bang

"The Big Bang, an intense energy singularity that created the Universe. But who created the singularity?" Francine mused.

"Who cares? I can't even 'explode' straight!" Walter looked at the minuscule cum stain on his boxers.

"Perhaps, I should call you Little Bang from now on..."

"You'll remove the triggers today, right?"

"Nope."

His torment continued...

Hypnotic Princess

"This is dumb!" Ashton grumbled.

"Are you serious?" Brianna retorted.

"Yes. What's the fun in setting traps and running around the same environments over and over again?"

"The fun is in unlocking new ways to win, like this Shiny Ball, here."

"What does it...?"

The screen flashed. Ashton served The Hypnotic Princess all night long.

Cumpelled

Xavier looked at Patrick in disgust.

"Please stop."

"I can't!" He jerked his will away. "The need to cum is irresistible."

"FUCK!" Xavier whimpered.

"Why are you like this, bro? It's my cock, not yours."

"You're not the only one Claudia hypnotized..."

A warm, white fountain spilled on the floor. No drop was left untouched.

Mindfuck Day

The spirals were lovely, yet headache-inducing. Two hours was long enough, and the weekend was waiting. Jonathan blinked and moved the cursor across the flashing screen to hit the "log out" button.

Immediately, his mind went blank, implanted trigger once more coming out to play. He could leave his Mistress' site, but never her control.

After the Movie

The movie credits faded to black.

"Awesome!" Karen said.

"I hated it!" Jake retorted.

"Why is that, spoilsport?"

"Because it's utter feminist drivel. Women will never rule the world. Oh, and mass brainwashing is bullshit, too."

"Is it?"

They stopped outside the theater. Jake glanced at a flashing billboard and kneeled to kiss her feet.

That Was Just Porn...

Her boots were walking all over his mind. Brandon heard each click, felt each painful stomp, and whimpered.

"God, what are you doing to me?"

"What you've always wanted..." His sister cooed. "Hypnotically enslaving you with my footwear."

"That was just porn..."

"... And now, it's real life." She concluded.

Brandon sank deeper under her control.

Priority

Gary cut the supermarket line much to the chagrin of all the other customers.

"What gives, jackass?" A redneck grumbled.

"I have priority!"

"Priority is for disabled or pregnant."

"What does it look like to you?" Gary rubbed his imaginary belly.

"It looks like you're either drunk or high!"

"More like hypnotized," Gary's girlfriend chuckled.

Irresistible

One hundred and forty-four bouts, one hundred and forty-four losses. Claude was livid.

"How do you...?" He spat. "You're so... tiny!"

Dahlia entered the ring, moving with the elegance of a belly dancer. Every move was hypnotic.

"I'm also irresistible."

He never saw the punch.

One hundred and forty-five bouts, one hundred and forty-five losses.

More Powerful

The shackled man screamed from the top of his lungs.

"You can't do this! I'm fucking Lucifer Morningstar!"

"Yeah, yeah, the big bad Mr. Devil himself." The platinum-haired woman in front of him laughed. "So what? I'm more powerful than you'll ever be."

"No mortal is more powerful than me!"

"Except a Hypnodomme..."

Lucifer gulped.

Conclusion

Well, was it tasty or what? Don't answer that, we both know the truth. However, don't think for a minute this is all. More fantasies than you can number are waiting for you on my personal website: https://www.sbspellbound.net so head there as soon as you can and feast yourself in all that's already available while wating for what's to come. Support my humble creative efforts if you wish to see more. Thank you in advance.